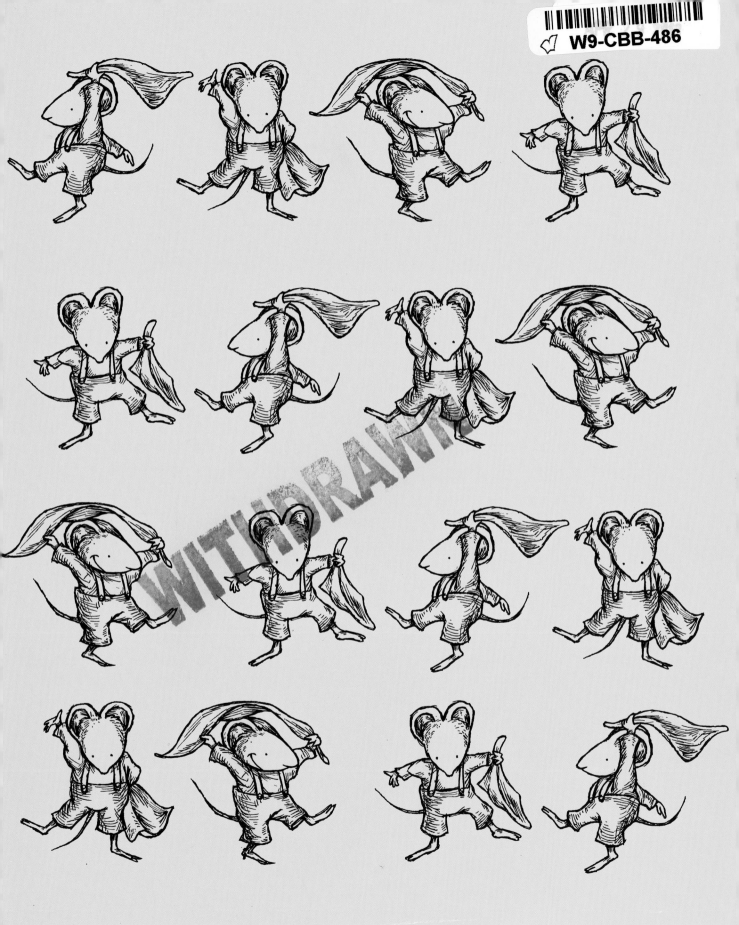

Owen

KEVIN HENKES

GREENWILLOW BOOKS

NEW YORK

FOR LAURA

Watercolor paints and a black pen were
used for the full-color art.
The text type is Goudy Modern.

Copyright © 1993 by Kevin Henkes
All rights reserved. Manufactured in
China by South China Printing Company
Ltd.
For information address HarperCollins Children's
Books, a division of HarperCollins Publishers,
10 East 53rd Street, New York, NY 10022.
www.harperchildrens.com

First Edition
11 12 13 SCP 30 29 28 27

Library of Congress Cataloging-in-
Publication Data
Henkes, Kevin.
Owen / by Kevin Henkes.
       p.   cm.
" Greenwillow Books."
Summary: Owen's parents try to get him
to give up his favorite blanket before he
starts school, but when their efforts fail,
they come up with a solution that makes
everyone happy.
ISBN 0-688-11449-0
ISBN 0-688-11450-4 (lib. bdg.)
ISBN 0-688-14886-7 (pbk.)
[1. Blankets—Fiction. 2. Parent and
child—Fiction.]
I. Title. PZ7.H389Ow 1993 [E]—dc20
92-30084 CIP AC

Owen had a fuzzy yellow blanket.

He'd had it since he was a baby.

He loved it with all his heart.

"Fuzzy goes where I go," said Owen.

And Fuzzy did.

Upstairs, downstairs, in-between.

Inside, outside, upside down.

"Fuzzy likes what I like," said Owen.

And Fuzzy did.

Orange juice, grape juice, chocolate milk.

Ice cream, peanut butter, applesauce cake.

"Isn't he getting a little old to be carrying that thing around?" asked Mrs. Tweezers. "Haven't you heard of the Blanket Fairy?"

Owen's parents hadn't.

Mrs. Tweezers filled them in.

That night Owen's parents told Owen to put Fuzzy under
his pillow.

In the morning Fuzzy would be gone, but the Blanket Fairy
would leave an absolutely wonderful, positively perfect,
especially terrific big-boy gift in its place.

Owen stuffed Fuzzy inside his pajama pants

and went to sleep.

"No Blanket Fairy," said Owen in the morning.

"No kidding," said Owen's mother.

"No wonder," said Owen's father.

"Fuzzy's dirty," said Owen's mother.

"Fuzzy's torn and ratty," said Owen's father.

"No," said Owen. "Fuzzy is perfect."

And Fuzzy was.

Fuzzy played Captain Plunger with Owen.

Fuzzy helped Owen become invisible.

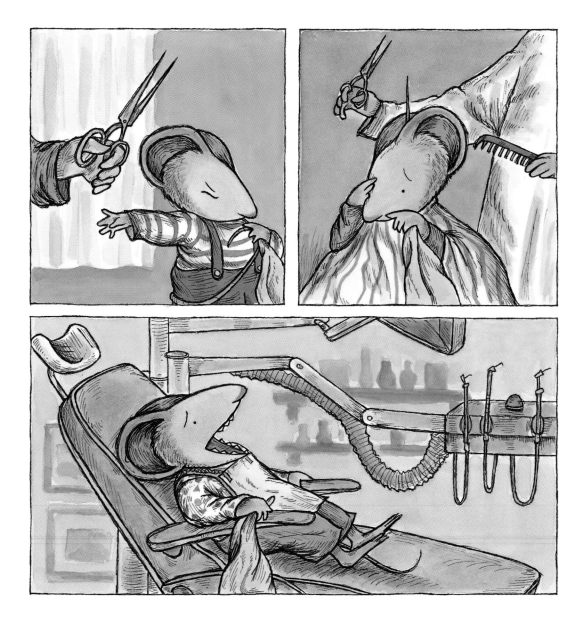

And Fuzzy was essential when it came to nail clippings

and haircuts and trips to the dentist.

"Can't be a baby forever," said Mrs. Tweezers.

"Haven't you heard of the vinegar trick?"

Owen's parents hadn't.

Mrs. Tweezers filled them in.

When Owen wasn't looking, his father dipped Owen's favorite corner of Fuzzy into a jar of vinegar.

Owen sniffed it and smelled it and sniffed it.
He picked a new favorite corner.

Then he rubbed the smelly corner all around his sandbox,
buried it in the garden, and dug it up again.

"Good as new," said Owen.

Fuzzy wasn't very fuzzy anymore.

But Owen didn't mind.

He carried it.

And wore it.

And dragged it.

He sucked it.

And hugged it.

And twisted it.

"What are we going to do?" asked Owen's mother.

"School is starting soon," said Owen's father.

"Can't bring a blanket to school," said Mrs. Tweezers.

"Haven't you heard of saying no?"

Owen's parents hadn't.

Mrs. Tweezers filled them in.

"I *have* to bring Fuzzy to school," said Owen.

"No," said Owen's mother.

"No," said Owen's father.

Owen buried his face in Fuzzy.

He started to cry and would not stop.

"Don't worry," said Owen's mother.

"It'll be all right," said Owen's father.

And then suddenly Owen's mother said, "I have an idea!"

It was an absolutely wonderful, positively perfect,

especially terrific idea.

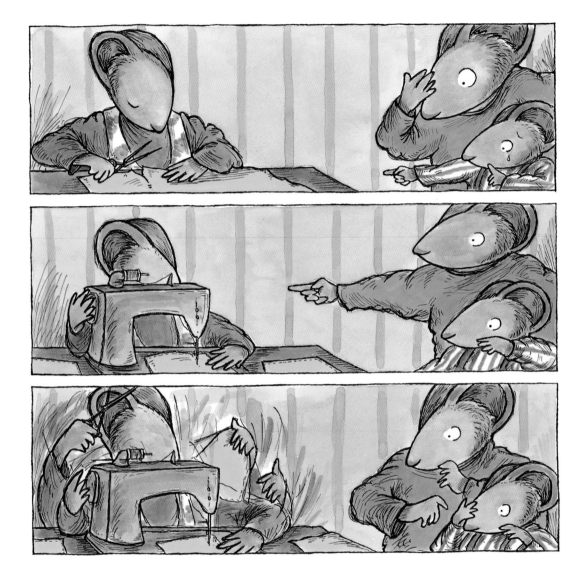

First she snipped.

And then she sewed.

Then she snipped again and sewed some more.

Snip, snip, snip.

Sew, sew, sew.

"Dry your eyes."

"Wipe your nose."

Hooray, hooray, hooray!

Now Owen carries one of his not-so-fuzzy handkerchiefs with him wherever he goes....

And Mrs. Tweezers doesn't say a thing.